THE ZACK FILES

The Boy Who Cried Bigfoot

LETTERS TO DAN GREENBURG
ABOUT THE ZACK FILES:

From a mother in New York, NY: "Just wanted to let you know that it was THE ZACK FILES that made my son discover the joy of reading...I tried everything to get him interested...THE ZACK FILES turned my son into a reader overnight. Now he complains when he's out of books!"

From a boy named Toby in New York, NY: "The reason why I like your books is because you explain things that no other writer would even dream of explaining to kids."

From Tara in Floral Park, NY: "When I read your books I felt like I was in the book with you. We love your books!"

From a teacher in West Chester, PA: "I cannot thank you enough for writing such a fantastic series."

From Max in Old Bridge, NJ: "I wasn't such a great reader until I discovered your books."

From Monica in Burbank, IL: "I read almost all of your books and I loved the ones I read. I'm a big fan! *I'm Out of My Body, Please Leave a Message*. That's a funny title. It makes me think of it being the best book in the world."

From three mothers in Toronto: "You have managed to take three boys and unlock the world of reading. In January they could best be characterized as boys who 'read only under duress.' Now these same guys are similar in that they are motivated to READ."

From Stephanie in Hastings, NY: "If someone didn't like your books that would be crazy."

From Dana in Floral Park, NY: "I really LOVE I mean LOVE your books. I read them a million times. I wish I could buy more. They are so good and so funny."

From a teacher in Pelham, NH: "My students are thoroughly enjoying [THE ZACK FILES]. Some are reading a book a night."

From Madeleine in Hastings, NY: "I love your books...I hope you keep making many more Zack Files."

THE ZACK FILES

The Boy Who Cried Bigfoot

By Dan Greenburg

Illustrated by Jack E. Davis

GROSSET & DUNLAP • NEW YORK

For Judith, and for the real Zack,
with love—D.G.

I'd like to thank my editor
Jane O'Connor, who makes the process
of writing and revising so much fun,
and without whom
these books would not exist.

I also want to thank Jill Jarnow,
Emily Sollinger, and Tui Sutherland
for their terrific ideas.

Text copyright © 2000 by Dan Greenburg. Illustrations copyright © 2000 by Jack E. Davis.
All rights reserved. Published by Grosset & Dunlap, a division of Penguin Putnam Books
for Young Readers, New York. THE ZACK FILES is a trademark of The Putnam & Grosset
Group. GROSSET & DUNLAP is a trademark of Grosset & Dunlap, Inc. Published
simultaneously in Canada. Printed in the U.S.A.

Library of Congress Cataloging-in-Publication Data

Greenburg, Dan.
    The boy who cried bigfoot / by Dan Greenburg ; illustrated by Jack E. Davis.
        p. cm — (The Zack files ; 19)
        Summary: After hearing stories that a Bigfoot-like monster is haunting Camp
Weno-wanna-getta-wedgee, ten-year-old Zack begins to find evidence that the legend
may be true.
        [1. Sasquatch—Fiction. 2. Camps—Fiction.] I. Davis, Jack E., ill. II. Title.
PZ7.G8278 B1 2000
[Fic]—dc21

                                                                                    00-027763

ISBN 0-448-42041-4   A B C D E F G H I J

Chapter 1

Do you believe in monsters? Horrible-looking beasts that are eight feet tall? Creatures that have fangs and claws and glowing red eyes and never brush their teeth? Most people think monsters don't exist. Most people are wrong.

Before I get too far ahead of myself, I should tell you who I am and all that junk. My name is Zack. I'm ten and a half, and I go to the Horace Hyde-White School for Boys. That's in New York City. My parents are divorced, but that was a long time ago.

The thing I wanted to tell you about started right after school ended for the summer. I had been working on Dad for some time about letting me go to sleep-away camp. My best friend Spencer was going to Camp Weno-wanna-getta-wedgee for four weeks. I wanted to go, too.

Dad said he was afraid I'd miss him too much. If you want to know the truth, I think *he* was afraid of missing *me*. But in the end, he gave in. Weno-wanna-getta-wedgee, here I come!

Camp Weno-wanna-getta-wedgee was in New York state, way up near Canada. To get there you had to travel on a bus for about a hundred hours. Early one morning in June, Dad drove me to the place where the camp buses depart.

It was a mess. It was so crowded you couldn't think. I didn't see Spencer. But I saw tons of other kids there with their parents and their duffel bags. There were girls there, too. Camp Weno-wanna-getta-wedgee has a girls' side right next to the boys' side. I saw two girls who live in my dad's building, Madeleine and Adrienne Ankuda. They mostly ignore me when they see me in the elevator.

They're both older than me. Adrienne is eleven, and Madeleine's twelve. Adrienne is a little taller than me and has brown hair. Madeleine is a lot taller and has blond hair. They both act like I'm about five years old. Still, Dad saw them and made me say hello.

"Uh, hello," I said. They turned.

"*Whoa!*" said Adrienne. "Like, look who's going to camp with us."

"No *way!*" said Madeleine. She didn't seem too thrilled about it.

"Well, at least he'll be in, like, the *little* kids' section," she said. They both walked off, because some guy with a whistle was blowing it and saying it was time to go.

"Well, Zack," said Dad. "This is a big step for you." Uh-oh! Dad was starting to get all teary-eyed on me. "But you're going to have a wonderful time. I just know it. Promise me you'll write often."

I promised I would. I managed to unhug myself from Dad and say good-bye. Then finally I spotted Spencer getting on one of the buses. I climbed on the same bus and squeezed in next to him. We were off!

The worst thing about the bus ride was discovering Vernon Manteuffel was on the bus with us.

Vernon is this kid from school who's a real pain. I thought I was rid of him until September. He brought all kinds of candy on board the bus and stuffed himself. Then he barfed all over the place. It was an awful sight. But not as awful as what I'd soon be seeing at Camp Weno-wanna-getta-wedgee.

Chapter 2

Camp Weno-wanna-getta-wedgee is in the middle of a forest of pine trees, at the edge of Lake Itchigoomie. The buses pulled up just as the sun was about to set. The big orange ball was ready to plop right into the lake. I had to admit it was a pretty cool sight.

Our counselors met us at the buses. Camp Weno-wanna-getta-wedgee tries to pretend it's a Native American camp, so the cabins are called teepees and the counselors are called chiefs.

"That's not politically correct," said Vernon.

"What do you mean?" I asked.

"You know. Calling cabins teepees and counselors chiefs."

"Oh, lighten up, Vernon," I said. I was praying Spencer and I weren't in the same teepee as Vernon. But no luck. We were all in Teepee Number Six.

A tanned guy walked up to us. He held a clipboard, and there was a whistle around his neck. He wore a Native American headdress with feathers.

"Welcome, braves," he said. "I'm Chief Marvin Wickroski, leader of Teepee Number Six. As soon as we get your bags put away, get ready for a cookout in the woods."

"Is there any poison ivy in the woods?" Vernon asked. "I'm very allergic to poison ivy. I have to take special pills if there's any poison ivy within a two-mile radius, even if I don't touch it."

"No poison ivy," said Chief Marvin, "but we do have mosquitoes the size of hummingbirds. And rattlesnakes, of course."

That cracked me up. Until I realized Chief Marvin might be serious.

The cookout was actually pretty nice. By the time we started, it was completely dark out. You could see fireflies and hear crickets. The campfire crackled and popped. We held long sticks over the fire and toasted hot dogs. We ate baked beans and french fries. We drank watery fruit punch called bug juice.

"I hear the bug juice is made from real bugs," whispered a younger kid named Josh Bloom. "Pass it on!"

For dessert there were s'mores. In case you don't know what s'mores are, here's how you make them: You toast a marshmallow till it's soft and runny. Then you put a square of chocolate on it. The hot marshmallow melts the chocolate. Then you clamp it between two graham crackers. I ate about seventy of them.

After dinner all the chiefs told spooky stories. The spookiest one was the legend about how a horrible creature lives in the woods of Camp Weno-wanna-getta-wedgee.

"It's hairy and about eight feet tall," said Chief Vinnie Mancuso. He was the chief of Teepee Eight. "It's got claws like a grizzly bear. And fangs like a saber-toothed tiger. And glowing red eyes. It has a fierce temper, and it smells like a garbage dump after a hot spell."

"What is it?" I asked.

"Nobody knows," said Chief Vinnie. "Some say it's Bigfoot. Some say it's Sasquatch. Some say it's a Yeti. Some say it's Chief Marvin. Ha, ha!"

Spencer raised his hand. I might not have mentioned it before, but Spencer is really smart. His IQ is around 1,000.

"Sasquatch, Bigfoot, Yeti," said Spencer. "They're all the same type of creature. Many people believe this creature is the missing link between humans and monkeys. In Tibet they call it a Yeti. In certain parts of America they call it Bigfoot. Native Americans call it Sasquatch. Nobody knows if it even exists."

Chief Vinnie seemed impressed. "That's right, Spencer," he said. "And thank you for sharing that with us."

"Has anybody at Camp Weno-wanna-getta-wedgee actually *seen* one of these creatures?" I asked.

"Not anyone who lived to tell about it," said Chief Vinnie.

"What's *that* supposed to mean?" I asked.

"I can't discuss it," said Chief Vinnie.

"Why not?" I asked.

"It's too horrible," said Chief Vinnie.

Then the camp director, Chief Herbie Flutie, gave out songsheets and we all learned the camp song. There were separate parts for Chief Herbie and the campers.

First Chief Herbie sang:

We're so glad you came to camp
Weno-wanna-getta-wedgee
Where your meals will all be cooked
By Chefs Bartholomew and Reggie

Then the campers sang:

Weno-wanna-getta-wedgee
Weno-wanna-getta-wedgee
We'll eat hamburgers or hot dogs
But we'll never eat a veggie

Then Chief Herbie answered:

You can hike or bike or snorkel

You can swim in Itchigoomie
You can water-ski or scuba
If you drown, then you can sue me

Then the campers sang:

We'll play basketball and baseball
We will skateboard on the jetty
Just be sure we don't get chewed up
By a bigfoot or a yeti

Then Chief Herbie sang:

You can munch a lunch of pizza
Or baked ham or pickled pigfoot
And I hope you don't get nibbled
By a Sasquatch or a Bigfoot

Then the campers sang:

Yes, we'll spend a super summer
Like Huck Finn or like Tom Sawyer
But if we're eaten you will hear
From our parents' high-priced lawyer

After the cookout, we all went back to the teepee. Spencer and I were in a bunk bed by the window. I let him have the lower bunk, partly because Spencer's my best friend, and partly because if a Bigfoot stuck a hairy paw in through the window while we were sleeping, it would be harder for it to reach the upper bunk.

When Chief Marvin turned out the lights, we lay in our bunks a long time, trying to sleep. I heard something outside in the woods. Something very big. Something making noises like an animal in trouble. A Bigfoot?

"Did you guys just hear something outside?" I whispered.

They listened.

"I hear something," said Spencer.

"Me, too," said a short kid named Casey. "You think it's a Bigfoot?"

"I doubt that any Bigfoot would come

this close to the teepee," said Spencer. "Maybe it's a raccoon."

Then I smelled a terrible smell. Chief Vinnie said one way you know there's a Bigfoot around is by its smell.

"Do you guys smell something terrible?" I asked.

"Yeah," said Spencer. "Pee-yew!"

"I smell it, too," said Casey. "It's coming from Vernon's bunk."

"I ate too many beans at dinner," said Vernon, moaning. "I must be allergic to beans."

"Oh," I said. That made me feel a little bit better. The stink was because of Vernon. But who had been making the strange noises outside?

Chapter 3

The next day was full of activities. There was swimming, boating, archery, and baseball. Vernon had notes excusing him from everything because of his allergies.

In the afternoon there was Arts and Crafts. That was one of the activities we shared with the girls' side. Madeleine and Adrienne, the girls from my dad's building, were making clay pots on the potting wheel. Madeleine missed the wheel and slopped clay all over my sneakers. She and Adrienne giggled like crazy. Madeleine said it was an accident, but I wasn't so sure about that.

The day went by really fast. After dinner there was a scavenger hunt all over camp for the boys. Spencer and I went together. Our first stop was the camp theater. We were supposed to find a red bandanna. We thought the costume closet was a good place to look. We didn't find any red bandannas, but we found lots of other cool stuff. I found a bearskin rug and put it around me.

"Look at me, I'm a grizzly bear," I said.

Spencer found some kind of an animal mask. It had long fangs and crazy-looking eyes. It was pretty spooky. Spencer put it on and made a low growling sound. He's really great at animal sounds. Even though I knew it was Spencer, it gave me the creeps.

"Hey, Spencer," I said. "You think this would scare anybody?"

"Maybe Vernon," he said.

"I've got a better idea," I said. "Let's go over to the other side of camp and scare some girls." It would be fun to get back at Madeleine and Adrienne for always treating me like such a jerk. "Do you know what teepee Madeleine and Adrienne are in?" I asked.

"I'm pretty sure they're in Eighteen," he said. "I saw it in Arts and Crafts on Squaw Goldstein's clipboard."

This sounded like more fun than the scavenger hunt. So I wrapped myself in the bearskin rug. Spencer put on the animal mask and wrapped himself in an old shag rug. We crept out of the theater.

It was already dark out. The moon was almost full, so I could see enough to walk without tripping. A patch of woods stood between the boys' camp and the girls'. We made our way to the other side of the woods in about five minutes. I don't know what we looked like, creeping through the woods in a bearskin, a shag rug, and that mask, but I wouldn't have wanted to meet up with us by surprise.

We waited until the girls came back. Spencer and I crept behind Teepee Eighteen and peered inside the window. The girls were mostly lying on their bunks, reading or talking. Madeleine and Adrienne were on the far side.

Spencer smoothed out my bearskin rug. I straightened his mask. Then we stuck our heads in the window, while Spencer growled as loudly as he could. Madeleine and Adrienne took one look at us and jumped three feet in the air. Then they started screaming.

"Bear!" screamed Adrienne.

"Bigfoot!" screamed Madeleine.

"Monsters!" screamed Adrienne and Madeleine together.

Other girls joined in. Pretty soon the whole teepee was screaming its lungs out.

We were laughing like crazy. We couldn't help it, it was so funny. I was laughing so hard, my bearskin slipped off. I think Madeleine saw my face before I dove for cover. Spencer and I ran back through the woods.

"That was so cool!" I said, gasping for breath.

"That was outstanding!" said Spencer.

"Did you see the looks on their faces?"

"I've never seen anybody so scared!" said Spencer.

We slowed down to a walk. We were sweating a lot. The forest was very quiet. You could hear crickets and other bug noises. You could smell pine trees and stuff. It smelled nicer than those cardboard room fresheners in the shape of a pine tree. When the wind blew, the shadows of the trees made spooky shapes in the moonlight.

"Hey, Spencer," I said. "Look over there. It's some kind of a cave or something."

We walked over to take a look. It was a cave, all right. It had a round opening about four feet across. It stank something awful. But Spencer stuck his head inside anyway.

"Wow!" said Spencer, holding his nose. "What is it?"

"Take a look."

I stuck my head in and looked. There was just enough moonlight to see by. Inside the opening was a weird arrangement of junk. Old sneakers. Empty graham cracker boxes. Rusty old cans of stewed tomatoes. An old tennis racket with no strings. Everything was arranged in a circle. I don't know why, but looking at it gave me the creeps.

"What the heck *is* this?" I whispered. I had to hold my nose, too.

"I think it's a den of some wild animal or something," said Spencer.

"Why do you say that?"

"Look at the stuff it's collected," said Spencer. "Look how the stuff is arranged. I think some wild animal doesn't understand what this human stuff is. I think it's trying to figure us out."

"When you say 'wild animal,'" I whispered, "would you, by any chance, be thinking...field mouse or rabbit?"

Spencer took a deep breath.

"No. Something way bigger than that."

"That's what I was afraid of," I said. "So what you're saying is, this is the den of a Bigfoot. And he could be coming home any minute now."

"That's pretty much what I'm saying," said Spencer.

Just then we heard something in the woods. A weird howl. Then a snapping and cracking of twigs. As if somebody—or something—was creeping through the forest. Something big.

"I'm out of here!" I said. I dropped the bearskin. I tore off through the woods.

"Hey! Wait for me!" called Spencer.

He dropped his shag rug and came racing after me.

We reached the other side of the woods in about a minute and a half. We hadn't seen the Bigfoot, but we weren't really looking for it.

When we got back to the teepee we told everybody about what we found in the cave. They didn't seem too impressed. I don't think they believed us. Vernon said he was allergic to caves.

The next morning at breakfast, Chief Marvin came up to me and Spencer in the dining hall. He looked really upset.

"You guys are in big, big trouble," he said.

Chapter 4

"**W**hat's wrong?" I asked, but I already knew.

"Did you and Spencer dress up as Bigfoot last night and frighten the girls of Teepee Eighteen?" asked Chief Marvin.

"Well, not exactly, sir," I said.

"Not exactly?" he answered. "What does not exactly mean?"

"Well, sir, I myself was dressed as a grizzly bear," I said. "I don't remember how Spencer was dressed."

"Chief Herbie has called a private

powwow to settle this," said Chief Marvin. "Come to Chief Herbie's office right after breakfast."

I was pretty scared. I guess it's stupid to be scared of anybody named Chief Herbie Flutie, but I was. Spencer didn't seem quite as worried as I was.

"Hey, what's the worst they could do to us?" Spencer asked. "I mean they're not going to make us wash the whole camp's dinner dishes for a week or anything, right? So why worry?"

The private powwow was pretty short. Chief Herbie told us our punishment. Spencer and I would have to wash the whole camp's dinner dishes for a week.

That night, right after dinner, we started.

"I don't think I'm going to like this," said Spencer.

"Me either," I said.

We began washing around seven p.m. It was nearly midnight before we finished our last dish. Spencer and I were exhausted. We could barely take off our rubber gloves and our rubber aprons and our rubber boots. We dragged ourselves outside.

It was another moonlit night. It was so bright it looked almost like daylight. From somewhere came an eerie cry. It sounded like a crazy person laughing. It sent shivers down my back.

"Spencer, what *is* that?" I whispered.

"A loon," said Spencer.

"Are loons...dangerous?"

"As dangerous as ducks," said Spencer. "Are you afraid of ducks?"

"Not that much," I said.

We walked into the woods that separated the main buildings from our teepee. The trees swaying in the breeze cast weird shadows in the moonlight. It made me pretty nervous. Probably because I was so tired from washing dishes. We dragged ourselves through the woods. And then I heard something. A low growl.

"Spencer, did you growl just now?" I asked.

"Just now?"

"Yeah."

"I don't think so," he answered.

We continued walking. Then I smelled a terrible smell.

"Spencer, did you make a terrible smell just now?" I asked.

"Just now?"

"Yeah."

"I don't think so," he answered.

Then I heard something behind us. The cracking and snapping of twigs on the ground. As if something big was walking behind us.

"Spencer, I think we're being followed,"

I said. "Let's get the heck out of here!"

We started running like crazy. Branches of trees whipped us in the face. I was breathing really hard. I was sweating. The faster we ran, the faster the thing behind us ran. It was gaining on us. Just a few more feet and we'd be out of the woods. We ran the last few yards. The last few feet. We were out of the woods.

"Help!" I yelled.

"Help!" yelled Spencer.

We reached the teepee. We tore open the door. We were breathing really hard. It was dark inside the teepee. Everybody was fast asleep.

"Wake up!" I shouted. "Bigfoot is outside!"

The lights came on. Guys were sitting up in bed, yawning and rubbing their eyes. Chief Marvin was pulling on his pants.

"What's going on?" he asked.

"Bigfoot!" I gasped. "It chased us back here! It's right outside the teepee!"

Chief Marvin grabbed a flashlight and ran outside. I thought he was really brave to do that. Maybe Bigfoots didn't eat chiefs. Maybe it was an agreement they had.

"Zack! Spencer!" yelled Chief Marvin. "Come out here!"

Uh-oh! Were we going to have to save Chief Marvin from the Bigfoot?

Spencer and I peeked out the door. Chief Marvin was standing there, poking his flashlight beam all over the place. Spencer and I crept out of the teepee.

"Do you see any Bigfoots?" he asked.

I looked around.

"Not that many," I said.

He gave me the flashlight. I poked it around all over the place. No Bigfoots. A bunch of the guys came out of the teepee. Finally, even Vernon came outside.

"I thought you said there was a Bigfoot out here," said Vernon.

"Well, there was," I said. "I guess he must've gone home."

The boys started laughing.

"There's nothing out here," said Casey. "There never was anything out here."

"There was so," I said.

"Hey, Zack," said another boy. "You ever hear about the boy who cried wolf?"

"So?"

"So you're the boy who cried Bigfoot."

Laughing, they all piled back into the teepee and went back to bed.

After awhile, Spencer and I followed them. We were both feeling pretty stupid.

"There *was* something chasing us," I said to him. "I know there was."

But how could we prove it?

Chapter 5

"Zack! Look at this!"

Spencer was on his hands and knees outside the teepee. It was early morning, right before breakfast. I walked over to where he was kneeling. He was looking at huge footprints in the earth.

"Aha! Proof at last!" I shouted. "Bigfoot was here! Let's go call the guys and show them. They won't be laughing anymore!"

"I've got a better plan," he said.

"What is it?"

"I'll tell you in photography workshop," said Spencer.

The great thing about photography workshop was that we always met in the darkroom, and they taught us how to develop and print our own pictures. The terrible thing about photography workshop was that Madeleine and Adrienne were in our group, too.

"Hey, everybody, look who's here," said Madeleine. "Bigfoot and his friend."

I flashed her a weak smile.

"I have to hand it to you guys," said Adrienne. "You sure did a great job on those dishes. I could actually see my face in my bowl at breakfast."

"Yuck, yuck," I said.

"You may think we're going to forget about what you did to us," said Madeleine. "We're not."

"Neither are we," I said.

I looked over at Spencer. He wasn't paying attention. He was pulling a big metal case off a shelf.

"What are you doing?" I asked.

"You'll see," he said.

Spencer took a camera out of the metal case. Then he took off the regular lens and put on a close-up lens. Chief Sheldon, the photography counselor, came over.

"What are you guys working on?" he asked.

"An outside project," said Spencer. "Can we borrow this camera and close-up lens?"

"Sure," said Chief Sheldon. "What for?"

"It's a secret," I said. I winked. I don't think I've ever winked before.

We took the camera to the teepee. Spencer and I searched the ground around it for Bigfoot footprints. We snapped pictures of the clearest ones. By the time we took the film back to the darkroom to develop it, everybody had left. That made it easier. Our next activity was woodcrafting. We figured no one would notice if we skipped it.

We blew on the negatives to make them dry faster. Then I made a print from the best one and held it up to the safety light.

"Wow, Spencer!" I said. "This is great! Nobody will ever doubt us now!"

"Let me see," said Spencer, reaching for the print.

"Hang on a second," I said. "Let me put it in the drier for a few minutes first."

"No, show it to me first!" said Spencer.

He snatched the wet print out of my hand. I lost my balance and crashed into a bunch of boxes. The roll of negatives fell into a pan of chemicals.

"Spencer!" I yelled. "Look what you made me do!"

We fished the negatives out of the pan. They were all splotched.

"They're ruined," I said. "Thanks a lot, Spencer!"

"I'm sorry, Zack," said Spencer. "But at least you got one printed. And it's the best one."

"I guess you're right," I said. "Well, now that we've got it, what do we do with it?"

"I think we should take it to Chief Herbie," said Spencer.

"Our biggest fan," I said.

"He's the only one who can give orders to have that Bigfoot caught before it eats anybody," said Spencer.

Chapter 6

Chief Herbie held the photo of the Bigfoot footprint for a long time without saying anything. Finally, he said something.

"Hmmmmm," was what he said.

"If you're thinking this is a joke or something like that, it's not," I said.

"Mmmhmmm," said Chief Herbie.

"Just because we dressed up like monsters to scare the girls in Teepee Eighteen doesn't mean this is a hoax," said Spencer.

"I didn't say I thought it was a hoax," said Chief Herbie. "Did I say I thought it was a hoax?"

"Actually," I said, "all you said was 'Hmmmmm' and 'Mmmhmmm.'"

"Correct," said Chief Herbie.

"So," said Spencer, "if you don't think it's a hoax, does that mean you think this is real? A real photo of the real footprint of a real Bigfoot?"

Chief Herbie let out a long sigh. Then he nodded his head.

"I have no doubt this is what you say it is," he said.

I gave Spencer a high-five.

"Great!" I said. "So what's our plan now?"

Chief Herbie opened his desk drawer and placed the photo of the Bigfoot footprint carefully inside it. Then he took out a key and locked the drawer.

"Our plan," said Chief Herbie, "is to tell nobody about this at all. Not a soul."

"OK, right," I said. "Secrecy is very important with something like this. And then what do we do? Call out the National Guard to surround the camp? Get guys with rifles to shoot it with special darts that knock it unconscious? Then haul it off to a zoo?"

Chief Herbie slowly shook his head.

"Then what?" said Spencer.

"Then nothing," said Chief Herbie.

"Excuse me?" said Spencer. "I don't understand."

"What didn't you understand?" said Chief Herbie.

"It sounded just like you said nothing was going to be done about the Bigfoot."

"That's correct," said Chief Herbie.

"Why not?" I asked.

"Because," said Chief Herbie, "all I need now is for there to be some big story about a Bigfoot here in camp. Every parent of every camper in the place is going to yank their kids right out of Camp Weno-wanna-getta-wedgee."

"And you'll lose all the money they paid you for the summer," I said.

"And what happens if this Bigfoot tries to attack some kid and eat him up?" Spencer asked.

"Oh, I don't think that's going to happen," said Chief Herbie.

"But what if it does?" I asked.

"Then," said Chief Herbie, "we'll do whatever needs to be done."

"What the heck does *that* mean?" said Spencer.

Chief Herbie looked at his watch.

"Oh, dear me," he said. "I'm afraid I have another meeting. But thank you so much for bringing this to my attention."

He got up and led us to the door.

When Spencer and I left Chief Herbie's office, we were both hopping mad.

"That guy," I said. "He's willing to put all of us in danger. Just because trying to catch the Bigfoot might end up costing him a little money."

"A *little* money?" said Spencer.

"OK, a *lot* of money. But what if some kid gets eaten? What then?"

"I don't know," said Spencer.

"If he's not going to do anything," I said, "then *we* have to. We have to prove there's really a Bigfoot out there. We have to get the kids to call their parents and make Chief Herbie do something about this. Before it's too late."

"You're right," said Spencer. "Unfortunately, our only proof of Bigfoot is that photo. And it's now locked inside Chief Herbie's desk drawer."

"Hey, we still have the camera. Let's go

take *another* photo," I said. "Let's go back to the teepee and get it right now!"

"You're right," said Spencer.

We hurried back to our teepee and got the camera. Then we tried to find the best footprint to photograph. We crawled around on the ground on our hands and knees.

"That's weird," said Spencer.

"What?" I asked.

"Not only can't I find a *good* footprint, I can't find any footprints at all."

"Me either. What's going on here?" I said. And then it hit me. "Oh no."

"What?"

"Chief Herbie beat us over here and got rid of all the footprints. Now we have zero evidence!"

Chapter 7

We tried to tell Chief Marvin and the guys in the teepee about what happened. About the photo of the footprint and the meeting with Chief Herbie. But when we told them the footprints near the teepee had disappeared, they just laughed at us.

By the time bedtime rolled around, neither Spencer nor I were in too hot of a mood. I lay on my bed a long time after lights-out. Thinking. I don't even remember falling asleep. But I do remember being jolted awake by an awful sound. A terrible moaning and groaning, like somebody in pain. Guys were snoring on all sides of me, so I guess I was the only one who heard it.

I hopped down from the upper bunk and walked between the beds. The sound was not coming from inside. I walked to the window and peered outside. I couldn't see anybody. Then I heard the sound again. It was definitely coming from outside.

"Pssst, Zack. What are you doing?" It was Spencer.

"I heard a terrible moaning," I said. "I think somebody's hurt out there."

"Should we wake Chief Marvin?"

"No," I said. "I don't think Chief Marvin would love to have us wake him up now. Let's just go see what it is."

"What if it's...?"

"Bigfoot? I don't know. I guess we should take something to protect ourselves."

We put on jeans, shirts, and sneakers,

and looked around for some kind of a weapon. We couldn't find a hunting knife or even a baseball bat. The best we could come up with was a badminton racket, and a big kosher salami that Vernon had hidden under a blanket.

We grabbed our flashlights, the badminton racket, and the kosher salami. Spencer grabbed the camera.

"In case we see anything," he said.

Then we crept outside. The moon was still pretty full, so it was bright out. We walked all around our teepee, scared of what we might find. We didn't find a thing. We didn't even hear the sound again.

"Might as well go back inside," said Spencer.

"Might as well," I said.

Just as we opened the door to the teepee, we heard it. A long, awful, tear-your-guts-out sound.

"It's coming from the woods," I said. "It sounded like it's really hurting."

"That could be a trick to get us to come into the woods," said Spencer. "So it can attack us."

We heard the sound again. "I can't stand listening to that," I said. "I'm going to go see what it is."

"I'm coming with you," said Spencer.

We walked into the woods.

It was much darker in the woods, but you could still see. We looked nervously in all directions. There was a slight breeze. I shivered, but not because I was cold.

And then we heard the sound again. It was very loud and very close, but we couldn't see where it was coming from. We started walking toward the sound.

"This is really creeping me out," whispered Spencer. But we kept on going.

Now we smelled a familiar smell.

"Unless Vernon followed us out here," I said, "I think we're about to see something that very few people have ever seen before. At least very few people who are still alive."

That's when we saw it. Not far away was a deep pit. The noises were coming from inside the pit.

"Where'd that pit come from?" I whispered.

"That's where the boys' old outhouse used to be," said Spencer. "That's what we used before we got toilets in our teepees. Something must have fallen into the pit."

The stink from the pit was worse than anything I had ever smelled before. Worse than Vernon. We crept up to the edge of the pit. It had been covered over with branches. Something must have walked on the branches and fallen through them. The pit was about twelve feet deep. At the bottom lay something huge and furry. Its

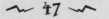

feet were the biggest ones I'd ever seen.

"Oh boy," I whispered.

"A real Bigfoot," whispered Spencer. "The missing link between humans and monkeys."

"This is really scary," I whispered.

"This is awesome," whispered Spencer. "We could become famous. The first people to catch a real Bigfoot!"

"We didn't catch him," I whispered. "He fell in the pit."

The Bigfoot gave another terrible groan. It shook the ground and made us jump about a foot in the air.

"We'd better get help," Spencer whispered. "The National Guard or somebody. But first we need a picture. So they'll believe us."

He aimed his camera and fired. The flash startled me. The creature looked up in our direction.

"Uh-oh," said Spencer. "He's seen us!"

"Me not only *see* you," said the creature, "me *smell* you. Pee-yew!"

"It talks!" I shouted. "I can't believe it! Spencer, did you hear that? It talks!"

"Of *course* me talk," he said. "How else tell what me want? Hey, maybe you help get me out of hole?"

"OK," I said. "Let's get him a rope."

"Zack, no!" said Spencer. "The minute we get him out of there, he'll eat us!"

The Bigfoot burst out laughing. "Eat *human*?" he said. "Ho, ho, that funny! Me never eat human!"

"Why not?"

"Human taste awful. Too stringy."

"How would you know that?" I asked. "Unless you ate humans, I mean?"

"Oh. Uh, me hear this around the woods. From grizzly bears. They say humans stringy. Get little pieces stuck between your teeth. You help me out of hole or not?"

"Well, I guess so."

"Zack! Don't do it! He'll eat you!"

"No eat human! Eat only s'mores and Ding Dongs."

"What if you're lying?" I asked the creature.

"OK. If eat you, then never believe me again."

"That doesn't work for me," I said.

"OK," he said. "If want eat you, could have eat you already many times."

"When?"

"One time when you running through woods, wrapped in bearskin. One time when you in my cave. One time when you coming home late from wash dishes."

"If you didn't want to eat us, then why'd you chase us?" Spencer asked.

"Want to say hello. Grizzly bears not fun. Grizzly bears tell stupid jokes."

I looked at Spencer. He shrugged.

"Look, Spencer," I said, "I believe him. I think he *could* have eaten us if he wanted to. I'm going to help him."

"Don't say I didn't warn you," said Spencer, hiding behind a tree.

There were no ropes in the woods. But I found a long branch that had fallen off a tree. I dragged the dead branch up to the pit and handed it down to the creature.

He propped it up against the side of the pit. He started climbing up the branch. Now he pulled himself out of the pit and stood up. He was at least eight feet tall. He stank to high heaven. He was so close he could have grabbed me. He didn't grab me. Then he did. He grabbed my hand.

"Yikes!" I shouted.

"I told you!" yelled Spencer from behind his tree. "Did I warn you or didn't I? Now he's going to eat you!"

Spencer took another flash picture.

"Let go of me, you monster!" I shouted.

The Bigfoot looked hurt. "Me just want to shake hands," he said. "Hello, boy. Me Freddy. What *your* name?"

"Freddy?" I said, shaking hands. "Freddy the Yeti?" I burst out laughing. Then Spencer burst out laughing. Then Freddy burst out laughing.

"I'm Zack," I said. "This is Spencer."

"Please to meeting you, Zack and Spencer," said Freddy. "Thanking you for get out of hole. Me do anything in woods for you. We friends for life. Maybe see each other in winter. Not much to do in camp all winter. Go to recreation hall, watch TV. Is how me learn to talk so good. Me like wrestling and info-mercials best. Tell, please—Girl Scout Cookies. These made from real Girl Scouts?"

"No."

"Good. OK, what now? You wish come to my cave, have lunch?"

"I've got a better idea," said Spencer. "Why don't we take you back to camp? We can show you off and prove you really exist!"

"OK," said Freddy.

"Wait, Spencer," I said. "If people find out we have a real live Bigfoot, Camp Weno-wanna-getta-wedgee will become a zoo. Reporters and TV crews will be running all over the place. Then they'll take him away. Put him in a cage in a freak show. He'll be locked up and miserable. We can't let that happen."

Spencer nodded. "You're right," he said. "Well, at least we have the photos."

We took Freddy back to his cave.

"Stay out of sight now," I told him. "We'll come back tomorrow night and visit you."

"Please to bring s'mores," he said.

Chapter 8

The next morning at breakfast, Madeleine and Adrienne came over to our table. They were giggling like hyenas.

"We heard somebody fell into the out-house pit last night," said Madeleine. "That wasn't you, was it?"

"No, not us," I said.

And then it hit me.

"It was *you* guys who made that trap!" I said. "You covered over the pit with branches so Spencer and I would fall into it!"

They burst out laughing.

"So who fell in?" asked Adrienne. "A Bigfoot?"

I looked at Spencer. Oh, did I want to blab about Freddy. But I kept quiet. Just before breakfast we'd developed the pictures. They came out great. If I showed them to those stuck-up girls, they wouldn't make fun of me anymore. But if I did that, then everybody would know about Freddy. The poor guy would be caught and thrown in a zoo or a freak show. It would be a horrible life.

"No," I said, "it wasn't a Bigfoot."

Spencer frowned at me.

"How come?" said Madeleine. "Is that because Bigfoots don't exist?"

"I guess they don't," I said.

I slipped Spencer a secret look. He sighed.

"The Bigfoot, the Sasquatch, the Yeti," I

said. "No one has ever proven that they exist."

"After lots of research," said Spencer, "we've decided they're imaginary creatures. Like unicorns or dragons."

Spencer and I looked at each other and winked.

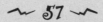

We visited Freddy every night after lights-out for the rest of our stay in camp. And nobody but us ever found out about him.

When I got back to New York, Dad asked me if I liked camp. I said yes. He asked if I'd made any new friends.

"Yeah," I said. "A really nice guy named Freddy."

"Well, maybe you'd like to invite him here for a visit sometime."

"Nah, I don't think that would work," I said.

"Why not?" Dad asked.

"Well, Freddy isn't like most of my friends," I said. "I mean he's nice, but he's kind of crude."

"A real animal, huh?" said Dad.

"Exactly," I said.

What else happens to Zack?

Find out in

How I Went from Bad to Verse

"**I** *wouldn't have if I'd stopped—*
I rhymed until I dropped," I said.

"Ah," said Dr. Kropotkin. "Well, that's different, if you couldn't stop. That's a different kettle of fish entirely."

"Have you ever heard of a condition like this before?" asked my dad.

"Hmmm," Dr. Kropotkin said. "Tell me, Zack. Have you by any chance been bitten by a tick?"

"*I thought it was mosquitoes,*
I got bit while eating Fritos," I said.

The doctor nodded his head.

"Rhyme Disease," he said.

"Rhyme Disease?" repeated my dad.

"*You mean it's like a sneeze?*
My rhyming's a disease?" I asked.

THE ZACK FILES™

OUT-OF-THIS-WORLD FAN CLUB!

Looking for even more info on all the strange, otherworldly happenings going on in *The Zack Files*? Get the inside scoop by becoming a member of *The Zack Files* Out-Of-This-World Fan Club! Just send in the form below and we'll send you your *Zack Files* Out-Of-This-World Fan Club kit including an official fan club membership card, a really cool *Zack Files* magnet, and a newsletter featuring excerpts from Zack's upcoming paranormal adventures, supernatural news from around the world, puzzles, and more! And as a member you'll continue to receive the newsletter six times a year! The best part is—it's all free!

✂ -

☐ Yes! I want to check out *The Zack Files*
   Out-Of-This-World Fan Club!

name: _____ age: _____

address: _____

city/town: _____ state: ___ zip: _____

Send this form to: Penguin Putnam Books for
                     Young Readers
                     Mass Merchandise Marketing
                     Dept. ZACK
                     345 Hudson Street
                     New York, NY 10014